Mr. Shipman's Kindergarten Chronicles:

FIELD TRIP TO THE FARM

by
Dr. Terance Shipman
Illustrated by
Milan Ristić

Forward

Field trips for kindergarteners are very special times. For many kindergarteners, it is their first experience traveling without their parents and away from their neighborhoods. I always loved taking my students on field trips. One of my goals was to make students' kindergarten year and exciting and memorable educational experience. The farm field trip was chosen to be our first trip because it was always one of our best trips. We would drive about an hour to Fayetteville, Georgia from Atlanta. The people at the farm truly made it a great experience. The students, parents, and teachers always enjoyed leaving the city to go to the farm.

Sincerely,

Terance L. Shipman, Ed.D.

Dedication

This book is dedicated to my grandparents, Bernie and Ruth Jean Davis. They have shown me nothing but love. Watching them loved each other is a continual example of how to love for me. Their love for their family has been unconditional. I thank you with all of my heart for your love and your example. I thank God for you both.

Love your grandson,

Terance L. Shipman, Ed. D.

1 Corinthians 13:13
"And now these three remain: faith, hope and love. But the greatest of these is love."

"Little brother, what are you planting in Mama's garden?"
Banicia asked.
"I'm planting some corn seeds we got from Mr. Shipman.
We are going to Ramsey Farms Friday," DeWayne announced.
"Wow! Now that was a great field trip when I went,"
Banicia said smiling.

"Wait, you're going to tell me another story, aren't you? DeWayne said.

"Yes, DeWayne. Don't you like my stories?"

"I love your stories, Banicia. Please tell me about your trip to the farm."

"Well, that day the classroom was full of excitement," Banicia began. There were parents and grandparents going on the trip with us.

We all boarded the bus headed to the farm. It was a long ride from the school to the farm.

We sang songs during the ride.

When we got there, we saw a huge sign held by a cow and a chicken. It said, "Welcome to Ramsey Farms."

A man rode up on a horse. He wore a big cowboy hat on his head.
"Well, hi Cousin Terance," said the man.
"Calvin, good to see you. Everyone this is my cousin, Calvin Barber."
"Hi, Mr. Barber," everyone said all together.
"Welcome to Ramsey Farms," said Mr. Barber.

My cousin, Terance well, Mr. Shipman here will take you around the family farms. Before I leave you, I want you all to meet my horse, Billy. Class say hello to Billy.

"Why did you name him Billy?" our friend, Joseph, asked.

"He is named after a famous Black cowboy, Bill Pickett. Billy, tell the class hello." The horse neighed and bow its head.

"Wow, that is so cool!" said Dewayne. "What happened next?"
Banicia continued, "We went through the cornfield maze,
petted the baby animals, and went to see Sallie."

"Who is Sallie?"
"She is the big cow we got to milk."
"You milked a cow?" DeWayne asked with wonder.
"Yes, and Clifford drank some of her milk," Banicia added.

We went on a chicken train ride around the farm. We saw the farmhouses, the barns, apple orchards, peanuts, vegetable gardens, and more animals.

We ate lunch in the main farmhouse. There was so much food, and all of it came from the farm.

"Class, it's time for us to go to the racetrack," Mr. Shipman announced.

One of our other friends, Summer, asked, "What are we going to see race, Mr. Shipman?"

"We are going to see pigs' race.

Our goofy friend, William, began to make pig sounds.

We rode the chicken train to the pig track. The pig races were fun to watch. The grown-ups went to the farmer's market, while Mr. Shipman took us to the playground.

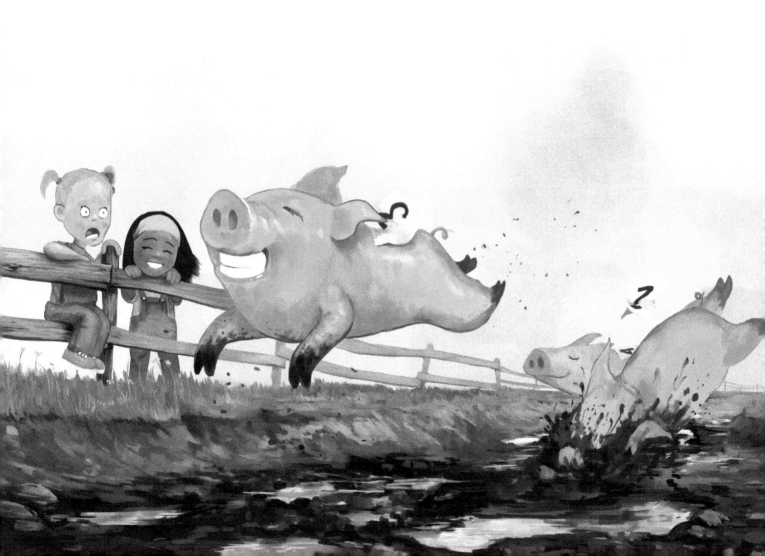

Mr. Barber and Billy were at the bus when we were about to leave. Mr. Barber asked our class if we had a good time. Tiffany answered for everybody. "We had a great time!" "I'm glad you did young lady," Mr. Barber said smiling.

We all received goodie bags filled with treats from the farms.
I sat next to Mr. Shipman and went to sleep.

"I hope to meet Mr. Barber and Billy when we go to the farm Friday. I have never met a real cowboy before," DeWayne said.
"I hope you do too little brother. And please share some snacks from your goodie bag with me."
"I will big sister."

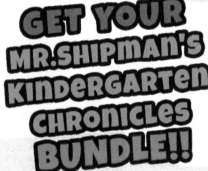

GET YOUR MR. SHIPMAN'S KINDERGARTEN CHRONICLES BUNDLE!!

Shop at www.teranceshipman.com

Mr. Shipman's
Kindergarten Chronicles

CPSIA information can be obtained
at www.ICGtesting.com
Printed in the USA
LVHW010744251121
704427LV00007B/385